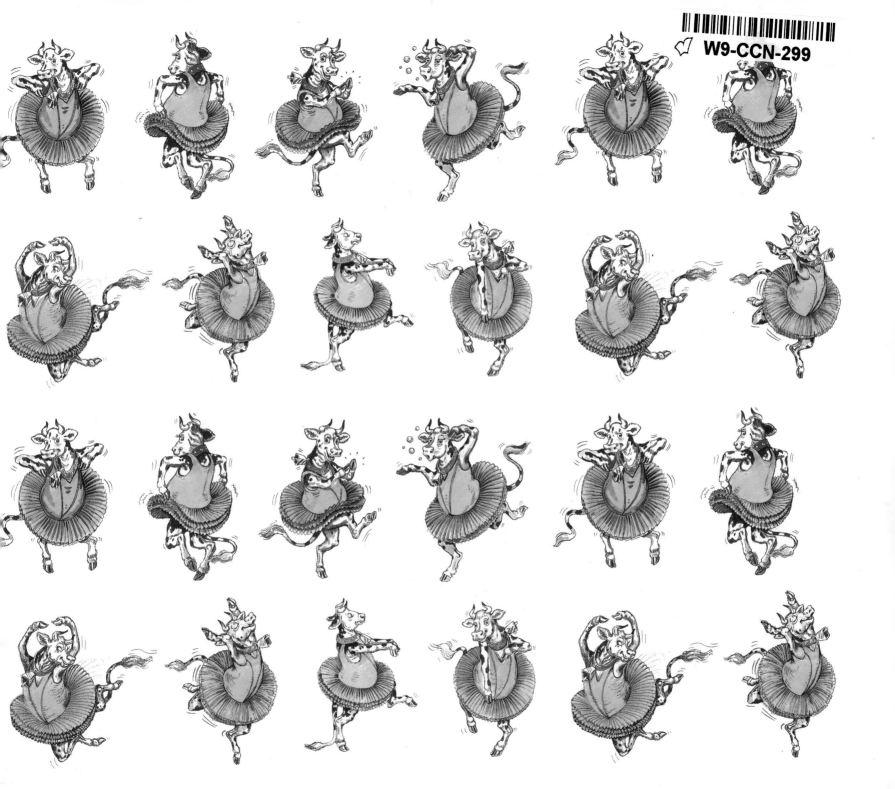

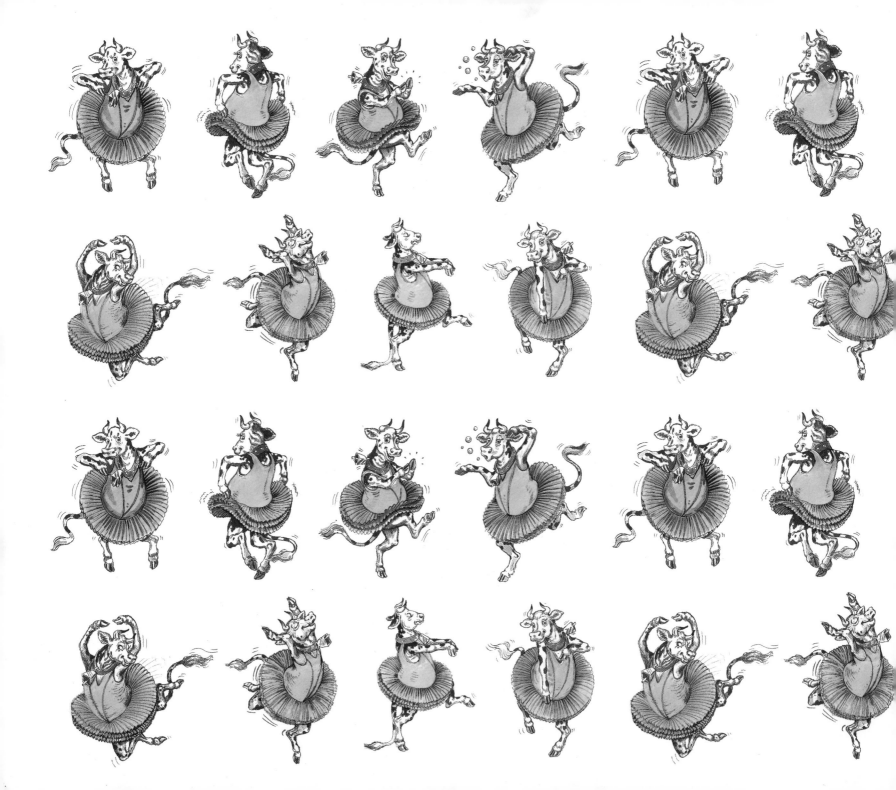

Gobble, Quack, Moon

To Sean + Justin, Blast off! Enjoy the journey!

Matthew Gollub

4.25.02

Written and Performed by Matthew Gollub
Pictures by Judy Love

Tortuga Press • Santa Rosa, California

Printed in China

Book design by Tania Garcia Design Studio
Book production by The Kids at Our House

The sound track on the audio CD accompanying *Gobble, Quack, Moon* was composed by Dennis Hysom of Compozarts, Sebastopol, California, and Matthew Gollub, with the exception of brief public domain musical quotations of "Thus Spake Zarathustra" by Richard Strauss (1864–1949) and "The Blue Danube" by Johann Strauss (1825–1899).

Publisher's Cataloging-in-Publication Data
(Provided by Quality Books, Inc.)

Gollub, Matthew
    Gobble, quack, moon / written and performed by Matthew Gollub ; pictures by Judy Love. — 1st ed.
    p. cm.
    SUMMARY: A host of barn animals cheers up Katie the cow by staging a ballet dance party on the moon.
    LCCN 2001130577
    ISBN 1-889910-20-1

    1. Cows—Juvenile fiction. 2. Moon—Juvenile fiction. 3. Domestic animals—Juvenile fiction. 4. Dance—Juvenile fiction. [1. Cows—Fiction. 2. Moon—Fiction. 3. Farm animals—Fiction. 4. Dance—Fiction. 5. Stories in rhyme.] I. Title.

PZ8.3.G6356Go 2002   [E] QBI01-700814

To my sisters, Joan and Elizabeth,
and to the children of America's heartland — M.G.

For Sue, barnyard sculptress and dance consultant extraordinaire.
And in memory of Harry, whose head was in the stars
and who remains most warmly in our hearts. — J.L.

There was a little barn that smelled of fresh milled grain
where the sun poked through after days of rain.
So out skipped four friends two by two, with a
Gobble-gobble, quack! Hee-haw. Moo-moo.

Gobble-gobble, moo-gobble, gobble-haw quack. Moo quack-a quack-a moo.
Just like that.

The green grass sparkled in the golden sun.
Splashing in the puddles sure looked fun.
The turkey jumped first. Then he hollered, "Let's race!"
But Katie the cow gazed off in space.

The good Farmer Beth waltzed across the yard
in her pink tutu and a leotard.
The donkey told his friends, "Let's flop in the hay."
But Katie watched Farmer Beth plié.

After dancing, Farmer Beth brought the feed sack by
with the corn and the barley piled up high.
"Katie, what's wrong?" said Beth. "Here's lunch."
The four barn buddies munch, munch, munched.

"The farm," said the turkey, "is the life for me."
"Hear! Hear!" The duck nodded. "I agree."

But when they settled down to sleep that night,
the stars above danced and the moon shone bright.
Katie gazed up at a shimmering star:
"I wonder what it's like to go away real far."

"Leave the farm?" screamed the turkey.
"Leave home?" cried the duck.
"Our life here's good." "Why push our luck?"

"Squish, flop, munch," Katie sighed, "all day.
There must be more to life than mud and hay.
I'd like to wear a tutu for a change of pace
and dance on moonbeams up in space."

"Dear friends," the old donkey began to bray,
"Katie's bored.
What she needs is a space ballet."

The turkey and the duck each knew a thing about flight.
They squawked and they quacked through half the night.
Then the four made a plan, and they talked, and they drew, with a

Gobble-gobble, quack! Hee-haw. Moo-moo.

Gobble-gobble, moo-gobble, gobble-haw quack. Moo quack-a quack-a moo.
Just like that.

The next day started with a *bang tat ting*!
The animals were building an incredible thing:
a tall rocket ship made of cans and glue,
while Farmer Beth slept in her bed with no clue!

"Ten, nine, eight—" quacked the duck.
"Wait, wait! I'm coming too!"
crowed the cockadoodle-doo.

"Seven, six, five, four—"
"Whoa!" neighed the horse.
"I've got to squeeze in too,
of course!"

Then the pig and the goat
and the kitten and the sheep
all climbed aboard in a big, hairy heap.

"Three, two, one!" "Roger."   "Blast off!" "Wee!"
And like *that* the green farm looked as small as a pea.

Gobble-gobble, quack! Hee-haw. Moo-moo.
Oink. Whinny. Meow. Baa. Cockadoodle-doo!

Gobble-gobble, moo-gobble, gobble-haw quack. Moo quack-a quack-a moo.
Just like that.

They landed on a surface full of Swiss cheese holes.
"Hey, who did all the digging?"
"Maybe big space moles!"

"Look at me!" Katie mooed. "We can float. No weight!
How fun! How neat! How udderly great!"

The whole crew played a game of duck-duck goosie....
Then they all jumped and danced the Watusi.

They did the mashed potato. And the zombie too.
Then the swim, then the fly, then they shimmied two by two.

Their dancing looked terrific.
No revue was ever greater
till a large ballerina landed in a tight crater.

"Heave ho! Pull!" neighed the horse. "One, two..."
Then out popped the cow, and she replied, "Thank moo."

"You know," Katie said, "deep space is fun,
but our Earth has grass and the moon has none.
And I miss the old barn full of fresh milled grain,
and I miss Farmer Beth and the sun and rain."

The donkey declared, "We need grains to munch.
Let's hurry home or we'll miss our lunch!"

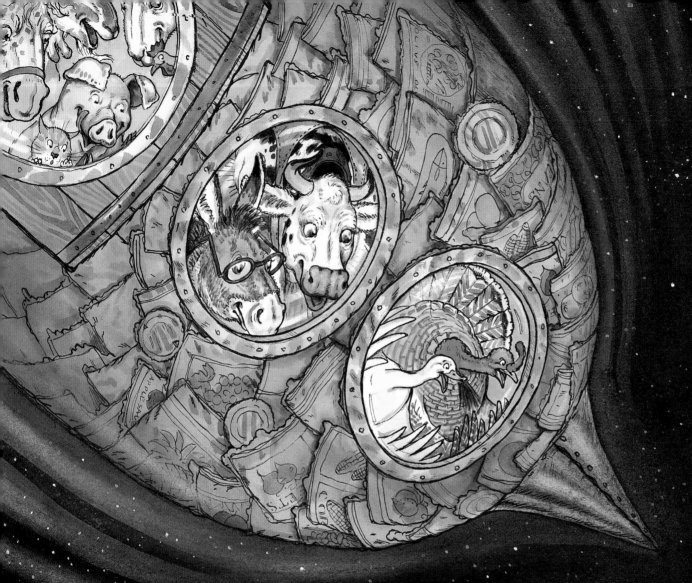

Gobble-gobble, quack! Hee-haw. Moo-moo.
Oink. Whinny. Meow. Baa. Cockadoodle-doo!

Gobble-gobble, moo-gobble, gobble-haw quack. Moo quack-a quack-a moo.
Just like that.

They landed on a
haystack beyond the rye
just as Farmer Beth
brought the feed sack by.

They ate with a crunch, slurp, munch, munch, neigh,

then squished
in the mud
and flopped in the hay.

The four friends yawned before sleep that night.

"This farm's the greatest!" Gobble! Quack! "That's right."
"Our life's the best life here or there."
"Our life's the best life ANYWHERE!"

"But still," Katie mooed, eying Mars,
"I'm sure glad we reached for the stars."

Oink. Whinny. Meow. Baa. Cockadoodle-doo!
"We are too!" agreed the whole barn crew.
Gobble-gobble, moo-gobble, gobble-haw quack. Moo quack-a quack-a moo.
Just like that.

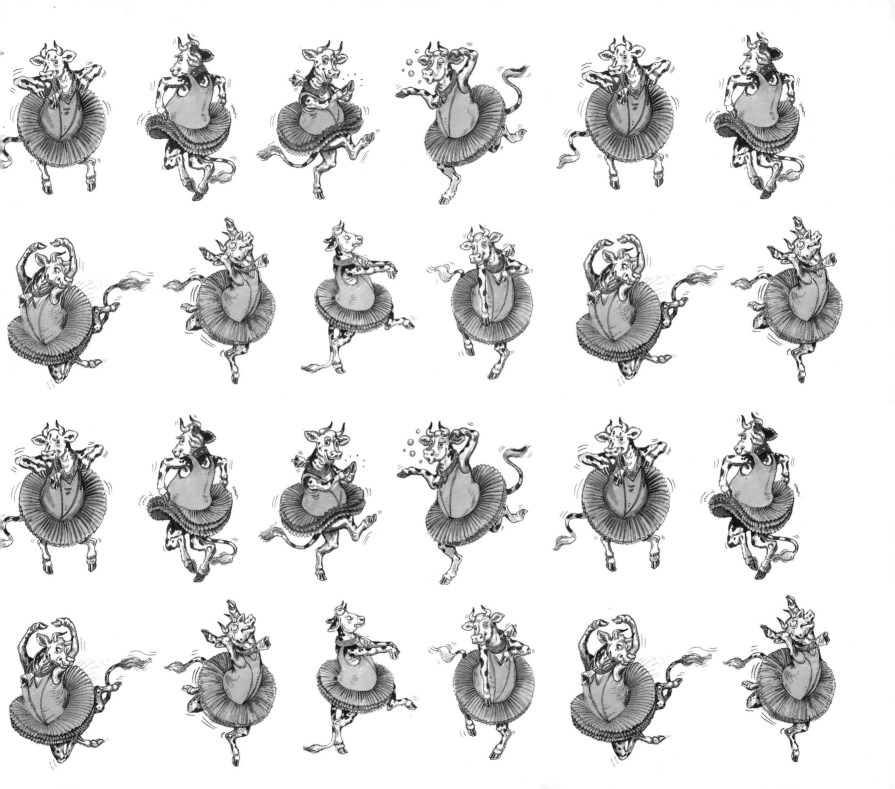

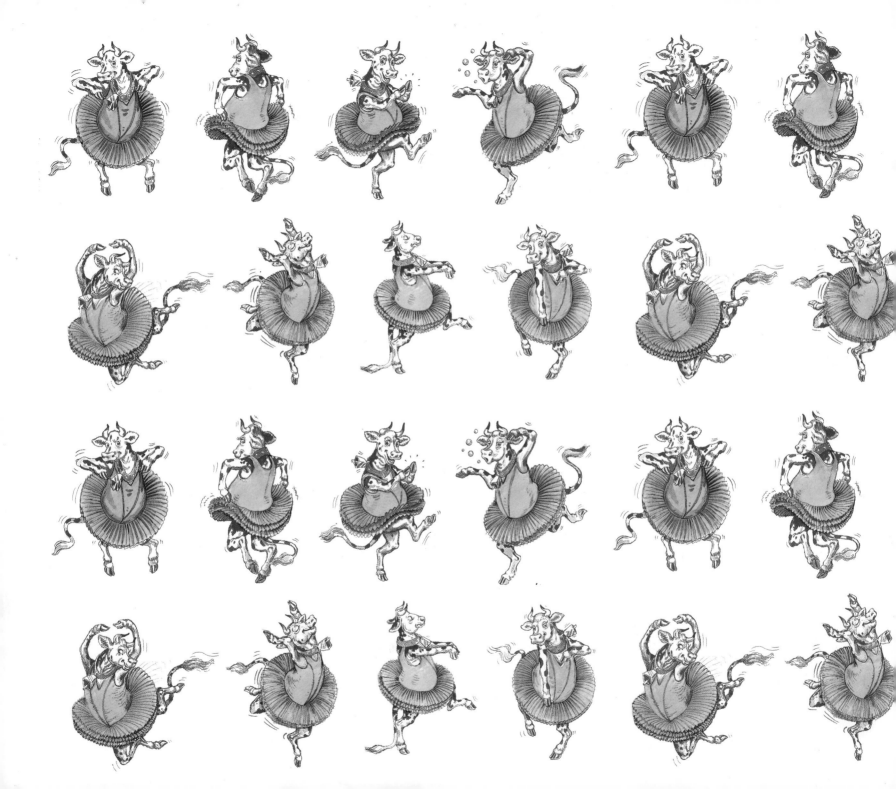